THE WAVES OF LO . _

Anthony Jones from a line study by the late
Lawrence Isherwood, FRSA, FIAL.

The Waves of Love

by

Anthony M. Jones
BD(Hons), FRSA

Illustrated by Louise Elliott

The Pentland Press Limited
Edinburgh · Cambridge · Durham · USA

First published in 2001 by
The Pentland Press Ltd.
1 Hutton Close
South Church
Bishop Auckland
Durham

British Library Cataloguing in Publication Data.
A catalogue record for this book is available
from the British Library.

ISBN 1 85821 847 0

Typeset by George Wishart & Associates, Whitley Bay.
Printed and bound by Antony Rowe Ltd., Chippenham.

Pictured at Tabhga, Galilee, September 1988, during the author's second working holiday at St George's Cathedral, Jerusalem.

Contents

Illustrations

Brief Biography

Anthony Jones was born in Southampton, educated at Emmanuel Grammar School, Swansea, and is a graduate of the University College of Wales, Aberystwyth (College of Welsh Independents) and a Postgraduate of the University College of Wales, Cardiff. He has studied theology at Westcott House, Cambridge and Harris Manchester College, Oxford, where he trained for the ministry, and is an alumni and Governor and a life member of the Oxford Union.

In 1992, he was elected a Fellow of the Royal Society of Arts, London. He is a Christian church minister and was inducted into the ministry at Bournemouth. Since then he has served ministries at Settle in the Yorkshire Dales, and is presently serving as Minister at Shotts E.U. Congregational Church, near Lanark in Scotland.

He is married to Beverley, and has one son, Samuel. His poetry was first published in *Modern Poets '81*, and since then he has had four volumes published *The Mantle* (1985); *Olympia* (1988); the anthologies *Warrior's Field* (1987) and *Celebrated Poems* (1990) were both sold nationally in aid of Cancer Research Campaign. His poetry has also been produced on stage at Aberystwyth and Cambridge.

'Set me as a seal upon thine heart, as a seal upon thine arm: for love is strong as death; jealousy is cruel as the grave: the coals thereof are coals of fire, which hath a most vehement flame.

Many waters cannot quench love, neither can the floods drown it: if a man would give all the substance of his house for love, it would be utterly condemned.'

The Song of Solomon, 8:6-7.

Acknowledgements

I am grateful for the encouragement I have received in early and recent years by the Lady Elizabeth Cavendish MVO, JP, and the Cancer Research Campaign in Great Britain whose support and belief in my formative poetic publications *Warrior's Field* and *Celebrated Poems 1980-1990* has spurred me on thus far.

For the indissoluble influence of my tutor and mentor, the late Professor D. Elwyn J. Davies (who gave me the title), and for the memory of those spiritual counsellors and divines who have fathered me along the path of life, amongst them Bishop Stephen Neill, FBA, Laurence Isherwood, FRSA, who provided the line study, Bishop W.G. Wheeler, the Reverend Alan Cole, and the Reverend Professor W.T. Pennar Davies (AberPennar), tutor and hymnwright.

I thank my friends the Reverend Andrew Gair and the Reverend Anthony Wilkinson for their loyalty and support. I cannot finish without thanking my dear wife Beverley for all her love, patience and belief in me. This book is as much to her as it is to all my loyal readers over the years, and indeed is a bequest to my family and future generations. Above all, it is dedicated to the memory of my own father, Ronald Jones, whose love of the English language was unsurpassed, always there as a friend and mentor, and a patient encourager of all my endeavours.

Dedicated to my father

Foreword

These poems are rich in both metaphor and aphorism. There are images here which will provide food for some very long journeys indeed; and deceptively simple reflections which I can well imagine readers extracting, scribbling on pieces of paper and carrying in their pockets. Something of Stevie Smith is evoked by pieces like 'Pilgrim Without Pew' something of R.S. Thomas in some of the short poems like 'Chapel Without a Cross'. But this is not to draw attention away from Anthony Jones's own very individual voice, which manages to be at various times lyrical, austere, highly traditional and sharply contemporary without losing its central focus on the interweavings of human and divine love.

Many of the poems also show a wit and nimbleness ('Oxford Riddle'), an ability to use rhythms and rhymes with lightness of touch, almost mischievousness ('Liberty') which intensifies the sense of aphoristic wisdom. The reader will often find far more sophistication than might at first appear. And the real and deep simplicity of 'Shining Through', 'Olympia VII' or 'To a Rose' is perhaps the most memorable of Anthony Jones's poetic registers.

Writing well and honestly about faith in our time is hard for theologians and philosophers, let alone poets. But it is all the more important to try – especially in poetry. Anthony Jones provides an excellent model of how to rise to this challenge. He writes about recognisable human reality, he writes *with* humanity – with wry humour, passion and exploratory patience; and he opens doors into vision. This is a welcome collection from a seasoned writer, and it will be one that the reader will want to return to. I have never heard Anthony Jones preaching;

but, on the basis of these pieces I can only imagine that a sermon from him would be a good deal more than the conventional experience of the pulpit. If the task of the ordained poet is, in a very special sense, to restore and reclaim a language that is in danger of becoming exhausted, reactive and flat, Anthony Jones embraces this calling with all his considerable skills and energies, and becomes a sign of promise about what can be done by others.

Rowan Williams
Newport, April 2001

Of Love,
Passion and Prayer

Lady Faith

Crushed and broken-hearted – love is crucified,
A heart flowers and fades through troubled days:
Just as my heart was beginning to open and
I felt I was becoming 'new',
She shut it tight and turned me against a cross.
The pains you wanted, I bore them for you,
That lady faith that did so much harm to me,
The harm that was so much love,
And now I see myself, as in a mirror,
I do the same to you . . . I am an orphan just
   like you.
Oh lady, sweet lady of faith,
Why can't we learn from each other?
You never loved me, that's more than clear,
But I am still here – in all my constancy,
A stranger whom you did not have eyes to see,
Yet, I still love you and you don't love me.
A vein you cannot sever,
Beauty will fade, but the heart of love is alive
   for ever.

I Yearn For A Heaven

I yearn for a heaven –
where there is no force to feed the frame,
Love's dying steps are heard behind –
the constellation of surprise;
And world's beyond the foreclosed eye –
the hands of God lay open wide.

I yearn for a heaven –
not on earth where men struggle with a fate,
For nothing can anticipate –
this other sight, this other sound,
Which cancels all we think we have found.

I yearn for a heaven –
where the gate is not closed,
For there is not room to presuppose –
just to sit and pray and be,
There is no other way to answer Thee –
I yearn for a heaven.

And I the feeble and indifferent man –
will seek to find, will seek to consecrate my will,
But peace be peace . . . and then shall sense be still –
and uncontrolled, undefinéd tears,
Flow freely from unfathomable fears – this is our lot –
well in this seed was sown – the mortal years,
I yearn for a heaven.

Liberty

The man of no chains – takes what he gains,
and moves within wheels within wheels,
like billows of clouds that fold for the sun,
A man of no chains has nowhere to run,
and nothing to hide but his heart.

Then moves the man of no chains
to trip the stair of signs,
as one by one bright saints appear,
A man of no chains makes his presence felt
in the centre of giving to living.

The man of no chains – takes what he gains
and reaches out into the darkness,
then by his glorious and golden glove
he grasps the gate of time,
Held fast by faith and all who will
find faith to hold his hand.

Immortal oath, hand carved in oak,
his face you will never disguise,
his voice you will hear
and in the garden of your dreams
he will reappear,
The man of no chains – takes what he gains
and tries to get the message through.

Dust and fair weather, sleep and demise,
Joy in the morning and tears in the night,
Virtuous freedom, cleverest and wise,
All who must join him have love in their eyes,
To be free and free indeed,
To forgive and not despise,
The man of no chains has naught and no reins
But the reins, of the reins of his heart.

Hymn To Walter Mitty

Only in the realms of fancy –
Dragons slain and maidens saved;
Candle-sticks and the cross,
Religion has what fantasy owns –
Breathing new life into old bones
Only in the realms of fancy –
Love conquers all
In the happy ending;
Only in the realms of fancy –
Then cursed the priest
Who lives for this
And makes the dream reality,
For he is not all he seems
He tells no man
What he has seen,
Yet, lovers love,
And dreamers dream,
Though gossips kill
The Spirit's flame.

Tarx̄ien

Waiting for the gods of men
Inscribed in sands of time,
Awake the soul, the sacrifice,
Have strength to draw the line,
Stir from the night
The blind of sight,
Make music for the heart,
Shine through the tears,
Dispense the years,
A life is in your hands,
Tarx̄ien, Tarx̄ien,
Search our eyes.
Tarx̄ien, Tarx̄ien,
Hear the cries,
Tarx̄ien, Tarx̄ien,
Search our eyes.

The Seagull

Sweet bird of grace, I see your face
Transfixed in time – o'er sea and space,
Sincerely sought through piercéd dreams
Of billowing clouds and fancied scenes;
Sleep soundly, safely, soon the sun
Will warm the heart, your cries make dumb,
Then swooping, gliding, footsteps sliding,
Pleasure borne by streams outshining,
Castle walls and cliffs dividing,
Childlike trust its source confiding,
All things flow from view;
Lap the waters, wave the shore
Of innocence and love made pure,
Fly back and face the finite hope,
The sunken treasures soon make float.

Pictured on 'Knightsbridge', a retired thoroughbred race-horse, Porth, near Aberystwyth, Summer 1985. (Photo: Malcolm E. Slater Photographics, Aberystwyth.)

Anathema

We none of us know – where we will go
beyond the blue tomorrow,
We none of us know – where we will go
when darkness fades,
And moon gives haze,
We none of us know.

The grey horse rides
Across the shore
of memory and something more,
And peace gives birth to twilight words,
Which slip and glide to depths inside,
For born again – man bears a sign
And passes like a whisper.

We none of us know – where we will go
and knowing none can know,
For he who has arrived – is about to leave
between twilight and the sun,
We none of us know – where we will go
beyond the blue tomorrow.

We passengers of golden dawn,
make music for a traveller,
No resting place,
No fount of grace,
But pearls beneath a sea,
For none can know – where they will go –
in sunshine or in shadow.

We can but hide – the tears we have cried,
And mirth will make its mark;
We none of us know – where we will go
But going we will go.

If We Can Love
(Obsequy)

If We can love
And leave behind ill feelings
Past transpire
To bring about this feeling
Here on earth –
a little smile,
a little pleasure,
a little mirth,
a little warmth
to lighten with the fire,
a little smile
to flatter nature's hour,
a little pleasure
to lift us from the pain,
a little joy
and laughter in the rain,
Then to live is not just to endure
if We can love.

In the great pulpit at Zion Church, Settle, Yorkshire Dales, where the author was Minister between 1994-1999. (Photo: Robert Lucas.)

Morpheus et Fabula

We trace the Creator's hand
in all things great and grand,
in nature's Master plan,
and crude imitation made by Man.
While genius tells forth
the glory of her art
And still, simplicity plays a part,
The quiet rambling of the frail at heart
in Sunday prayers,
Little gifts to God,
The moving sound of falling rain
For all that's born
is born from pain
and tears, the darkness of disdain.
Hidden, undiscovered virtue
Cries for lack of love,
And lost innocence
For want of gain.
The timeless time.
The happy days
Of bucket and of spade
Drawing pictures in the sand,
We trace the Creator's hand.

Ivory Towers and Dreaming Spires

18th century engraving of Oxford from the north. Harris Manchester College, Oxford now stands on the site of the cornfield but the buildings just beyond it are occupied still by the College and they are carefully preserved. The old stables, some of which still stand, some of which were replaced in 1974 by Vaughan House and some of which have made way for the Adrian Boult Music Buildings, can be seen just in front of St. Mary's spire and the Radcliffe Camera.

Latimer's pulpit at St Edward King & Martyr Church, Cambridge, circa 1510, from where the young poet preached as a student. The church is a 'royal peculiar' and has historic links with Trinity Hall, Cambridge. F. D. Maurice, a renowned liberal Christian thinker also had a notable connection with the church.

Pilgrim Without Pew
We Are Despicably Indisposed

We are, so we are told, so despicably indisposed
to all that's 'good',
But for love of all those 'debs' and graces
in their Ascot hats,
We are despicably indisposed
by lack of virtue,
Blest communion without call of bells,
'To pass our time in rest and quietness'
Without smell of incense, perfume,
lipstick and now the collar,
or, pious preachers' platitudes.
But, the ladies, ah! the ladies!
Were it not for them,
We are despicably indisposed.

We are despicably indisposed
by afternoon tea and muffins at the Ritz,
Desirous of all things worldly, sane and just,
We have little need to feel we 'must',
We are despicably indisposed,
Bereft of duty, devoid of care,
save that towards fellow man and members of the 'Club',
We are despicably indisposed.

We are despicably indisposed
by cocktail party, cultural pursuit,
by Opera, Theatre, Music, Poetry,
The language of the soul,
We are despicably indisposed
by garden party, champers, cigar and toast –
'To friends both near and far'
And foreign parts by plane not car!
We are despicably indisposed.
We are despicably indisposed,
And have no regrets, save marmalade, tea and toast,
And the quiet walks with dog whom we love most;
Ah the freedom, ah, the greatness, ah, the release!
No more the labyrinthine passage-ways
Of book and pen,
Chained to desk and chained to Men,
We are despicably indisposed.

We are despicably indisposed
by the company of those we love the most;
We are a society, not a church,
We are despicably indisposed.

Pictured with the Reverend Anthony Jones at his induction service in Bournemouth, June, 1992 are left to right; The Reverend Ralph Waller, Principal of Harris Manchester College, Oxford, the Reverend Dr Frank Schulman, the Reverend Dr Dudley Richards, the Reverend Dr Duncan McGuffie.
(Photo: Courtesy of Southern Newspapers Group PLC.)

Oxford Riddle

'Twas Oxford in Autumnal leaves –
And more than leaves which fell were these;
Great scions of the ivory towers
Whispered murmurings of misdeeds,
'Twixt cocktail party, Bishop's grin,
"Twas a devil of a thing to mix with gin!'
Honoured Fellows, celebrated Inn;
'Eagle and Child' and sherry laced
By delicate hand of a Master's grace.

Cry scandal! Danger! Watch your words!
My head is buried – 'tis quite absurd!
Randolph, Carfax, Covered Market,
Caught in Catte Street
Where walls seem far from it,
Renewing books as winter draws on,
The constant round, and round after round;
The cornflakes, the toast and the yoghurt.

Polite conversation amidst murmurings of war,
And rushing to chapel for prayers;
It's about time something was done
About the carpet too!
Someone may trip unawares!
Consider it done – there's spice in the rum!
The Fresher is not a well fellow,
We run for our gowns as the gavel does down,
And the smile on the Master's wife.

As a cause of some hilarity
Our ties wear thin with charity,
We wait and we wait,
Sometimes Christmas comes late,
Notwithstanding the gate, which has been tried;
We have scaled the wall,
And nobler ones fall.
But nothing can keep us at bay,
The world is our oyster
(And a weekend away),
The College, the keys to the door.

Love's Fading Light

In Loving Memory of Prof. Gareth Bennett
Fellow of New College, Oxford   RIP

We met though briefly over sherry at Pusey,
A nonchalant smile, and warm and friendly words
of Wales, the native land and weather,
Mary Mags, a stone's throw away,
is where we left our gowns.
Shrines of High Church hymnary and flowers;
The noblest of men, the finest of scholars;
The pen is the sacrifice in a world such as ours.

Last goodbyes from clerical windows, ivory towers,
from all the precious minds he touched and oft inspired;
This man, an earnest soul, an erstwhile saint –
has left a legacy to respect.

The words remain, the power of words,
indelibly etched upon All Souls, fellows, dons;
Conviction knows no bounds,
its limits endless.

Hail, blackest night!
Love's fading light
is then reflected.

The author with his father Ronald Jones, B.Com at the alumnis celebrations, Harris Manchester College, Oxford, June, 1992. (Photo: Gilman & Soame, Oxford.)

New Songs,
Old Loves

Father, Dear Father

In Loving Memory of my father, Ronald Jones

A word of advice to all who would fall,
Remember your father's words,
And never forget the example he has set,
The spirit with which it was done.
Look upwards, thank goodness
For all that he knows,
And all that he passes on.

Who is always there
In the next chair,
Who taught us our first few steps to walk
And spelt our names before we could talk.

And father knows best,
You can keep the rest,
Friend, friend, dearest friend,
Greatest and best,
Redoubtable to the end.

Goodbye, But Do Not Cry

Goodbye, but do not cry –
The love we shared together
Never meant much to you nor I;
The memory of joy and grace
Is thus erased without a trace,
The day is gone,
The night has come,
The dress you wore
While just for fun;
And tears no longer hide
Nor mark the warmth inside.

The hand that lost the glove
   is smitten,
The heart that bore the weight
   released,
The voice that broke, though calm
   still speaks,
Eyes gently watering
   in mind's solemnity,
Say, say goodbye, but do not cry
The love we shared together –
never meant much to you nor I.

Say goodbye, but do not cry –
'It's what you want that counts';
But still, still you pierce me through
And whisper through the gloom,
I'm in your room, I'm at your side,
I am Love's Immortal Bride.

Joie De Vivre

Someone so wonderful,
Someone so young,
Should not be so sad,
Worrying about things,
As if all were so bad

Life is a gift too precious to waste
Nothing is never, if ever worth haste,
Laugh while you can and treasure the sun,
All that we do may never be done,
The tracks of the race are still being won.

The wheel still in spin is still being spun,
The journey we travel – we travel through time
With no need for a star and no need for a sign;
Latch on to the moment and make of it fine,
The rhythm, the spirit, the sense of the rhyme.

World Without End
(Epitaph)

When we die – we die without reason
and fly to unknown worlds
other than this.
Or is it just that we leave behind us,
naught but dust and fair weather.
A myriad of memories – for they will
outshine us.
A few little thoughts for loved ones,
and then we pass on.
Farewell, brave world, for I am gone,
I've naught but your prayers
to hang my hat on.

Llanbadarn

At the breaking of the bread
        His Spirit speaks through
In the silent nights of souls
        His Spirit speaks through
In the quiet 'God Almighty',
        His Spirit speaks through
In the flowers having faded, in the worlds having flown
In the dawn having woken – in all else
that is left unspoken still
        His Spirit speaks through

In the trees that part their branches – sweeping
through infinity – So with us He reaches
outwards, upwards, downwards, inwards
pulsing through the roots of life,
So always ever a sleepless whisper
        His Spirit speaks through;
Yet do I doubt Thee, yet do I trust Thee,
at the closing of the day – for a baby's born
tomorrow – and another new life is on its way

At the beginning and at the end His tears break
through our blinded vision – in our moments of
utter despair –
        His Spirit speaks through

Yet will I alway ever remember, yet will I alway never forget
the brink you brought me to,
For it is love that takes us there –
        and His Spirit speaks through

St Germaine

Paris '86 (To Aicha)

She is the queen
the dream
the silhouette
the moon her pillow
the streets are her disguise
she wipes away the tears
you can not cry
you fear her whisper
'let me close your eyes',
but, fears unfounded flee in paradise;
let me close your eyes,
at dusk you meet her
silent-trip the stair
celestial voices sing above –
'to all those whose hearts remain
unmoved by love'.

'Postcard to the past' –
'O might we return to an England – once green.'

Tryst

Poem to a bride on her Wedding Day.

Once more with me – the green fields wander my lady of the Lea
As step by step we wind our way in patient pleasantry,
Once more the green fields wander with my lady of the Lea
Was I the one that bore the cup before the maiden's lip?
Was I the one that bore the cup, who desirédst thee?

And hand in hand the green fields wander with my lady of the Lea
Who burst bright joy into the night – the lady of the Lea
for 'love grows with experience' quoth she,
A shepherd king has gone before to set the spirit free,
At heaven's gate we pledge our hearts in God's sweet reverie.

Publicity still for 'Warrior's Field' (the land we left behind): Selected Poems, published in 1987.
(Photo: Malcolm E. Slater Photographics, Aberystwyth.)

Death and Remembrances

a. L. Elliott

Warrior's Field

The grey-coat strangers steal to die on warrior's field
The night before the storm the valiant sleep
With each one the thought of victory – be he slain
    on warrior's field.

And heaven's whispers light the skies,
    for mortal ears – immortal cries
On warrior's field a stranger too was I
    born from pain, I crushed the blood-stained wire
Far from the forest of human desire.

And so we conquered higher plains as tears triumphant fell
Then was that land we left behind a heaven or a hell?

For though the bugle morn resounded – none could hear,
As brave hearts fought and brave hearts died,
And thus it was for both our sides,
Each man about his business, caught up, confused and blind.

The banner in ashes, barely reads the sign:
    'No man here will he rest find
    death like a whisper heeds her call
    then sleeps the silent mind'.

Shining Through

To step out of the mortal frame,
To see life and feel no pain,
No shame, no shame
Though forever in our midst
The serpent sits.
A candle glows.
The books are closed.
No mind made manifest behold
That unseen state beyond the flesh.
Forever pines the heart
As with things that cannot be,
O, how precious are the things we cannot see
As in the day the stars are shining.
Then turn again the smiling face,
Look into the sun, receive its rays.
Experience the wonder of creation
Where no man can forget
Sunrise, sunset.

Despair

O, where is she now, my fair One?
Hankering in someone else's arms,
Whose love I know was sacrificed
Upon the cross of self-destruction,
Whose heart touched mine
Across the millions of miles and dominions,
Whose lips touched mine –
And death lay sleeping out of sight,
And no prayer could bring her back . . .

An extract from the stage play *The State
of Love* performed at the Theatr Y Werin,
Aberystwyth on 5 May 1986.

Pictured with son Samuel, October, 1998.

Rhapsody

To my son Samuel
Born 25th July, 1998

My eyes lifted and I was in heaven
Behind the pool – where everything was green and glorious
And hearts held hands and lovers kissed at sunrise.
The dream was dreamed, and dreaming youth stood still,
Where moon was bright and sun was gold,
Of cherry lips the story told – the fastest heart is captured,
For to grow old is to glisten, but innocence is wisdom.

Chapel Without A Cross

An offence to the Chapel
that bears no cross,
And demands not the glory of men
For love was the crime –
cast out with the sign
The Word,
for words again and again.

How Fair The Face
(To Emma)

You were behind the dream,
the arranger, the inconsequent mover,
the well-founded face,
the friend, believer, lover,
crosses the cobblestones,
the heaven all my heart owns.
My little corner of the world –
My treasured grace –
How fair the face?
How fair the face?
How fair the face?

Emmanuel Schooldays
(1969-1974)

Where are they now! It seems so long ago,
Those wayward days of boyhood youth
Crossing Mumbles Road through Emmanuel's 'Jungle'
And rushing for buses and morning prayers
Up the old railway-line –
And 'short-cuts' if we were lucky,
On cross-country runs!

Where are they now? It seems so long ago.
But the vision is clear of the teachers we loved,
The caring Mr Lee and the gracious Miss Rush
With whom we first celebrated 'life's creation'
   with a brush,
Mr Bruty taught us 'sport' and Mrs Mandeville
   was always 'French'.

Mr Brent the 'woodwork' master
   was skilful with his chisel.
With him we crafted dove-joints, chairs, book-shelves,
   lampstands, bureau-doors,
And most remembered film-shows
Which he gave to all the 'boarders'
'Foxhole in Cairo', I remember –
Films were never 'out of orders'!

Where are they now? It is difficult to remember
But, as my memory fades with age,
I summon up my pen and write
What's best captured on the page.

Where are they now? If we could but remember,
For as in study we find the soul's contemplation,
It is hard to recreate the same sensation,
Of burning hearts, brave jubilation and striving
    towards the goal,
For school-boy crushes are stronger than the pen,
And stirrings in the soul.

Where are they now? If we could but remember,
Just the idylls of a dream,
Pictured innocence and beauty
captured in the mind's eye,
Christine, Theresa, where are you,
Who were in my class at school?
The best friend with whom, alas!
We shared the first cigarette,
Where are they now, where are they now?
As if we ever could forget.

Publicity still for 'Olympia', published 1989, pictured at Westcott House, Cambridge, June, 1989.
(Photo: Courtesy of Dumbleton Studios, Cambridge.)

Olympia I

On earth the trembling footsteps sign the vow
For first we meet in heaven then in hell
A finitude of virtue knows us well
The cloistered arches bind us to the spell;
and naught will wipe away the tears of glory now
The struggling figure stands before the sign
This world portrays the pleasure and the pain
so whispered saints behind us in their train
But, look beyond, 'tis treasure in the hand
That catches rain.

II

Look not with sorrow on thy life,
nor mar the noble path of chance
that indiscretion used,
for chance would seem too fine to hold
its fleeting breath dies with the soul
But, memory instils the line,
portrays a virtue,
grasps the vine
Its leaves will never blossom out of time,
The light which darkness hides behind,
Your glass-like tears poured out of wine
And, cup-like hands incline.

III

You came from nowhere bringing love to lives
This precious heart – this precious soul treads by,
Then meet between the boughs – the mellow mead belie,
Engraved, a name that stands always
A name, her name – a love have I
For beauty has such sweet disguise
And mirrors reason in her eyes
And once a word is read – there rings the bell
O, Olympia, Olympia fare thee well

IV

There on the shore – the spirits live
An empty sea-bed, where only ghosts of lovers play
Lie tempted by the light of day –
Asleep, the bitter-sweet,
The memory of love we made
And turn our backs on all that we once knew
For sticks and stones may break our bones
But, words can cut us through
So none may fall – where all have fallen excel
O, Olympia, Olympia fare thee well

V

The stone becomes the shadow –
For it is the sun that teaches
Leaves us dust and ashes,
Blood that bleaches;
So paint becomes the picture;
Drawn from life her creature
Incidental death, a reckless preacher
Catching unawares – for none can tell
Olympia, Olympia fare thee well.

VI

Remove the stain from mortal men
the toil from human race,
The memory of another time
becomes another place,
The memory of a person slips
into another face,
But, still the hand carves out
the name on slate
We pass from time to time
and lose our way,
For feelings draw us closer
only words can tell,
So mind the invisible hero
winds the well,
O, Olympia, Olympia
fare thee well.

VII

Love draws us to love
the greater goal,
She has left her tracks
upon our souls,
Allows us space to enter;
hands that heal,
But more than this
the greatest pain
is one you cannot feel,
Between fast-fading moments
release is sure,
Her pale-illumined hands
bring you to see,
Eternity in memory
is the key,
Life draws from life
and so may we,
The higher state
beyond the flesh
its shell
Olympia, Olympia
fare thee well.

Meditations

Set No Flame (To Thy Face)

Sacred to the memory of a true and lasting love

Set no flame to thy face –
And the bold hand that made thee
hold thee true;
Let no hurt or harm come near,
Then with thine angels disappear.
Fear not fortune, fly from fame,
What is best in life will still remain.

Set no flame to thy heart –
nothing on earth must keep us apart,
The love that gave you –
gave your love;
And the sparrow will still fly –
Though we are dead and so die.
Still we be the garden of truth
we have known.

Set no flame to thy hands nor thine arms,
In another life we'll still embrace,
And though untouching – we will touch;
As children clasp the hands of those they love,
And reaching from beyond – we'll touch
the hands of centuries.

Set no flame to thy legs nor thy feet,
For where they have trod no other went before,
And no other has since been.
So beautifully encompassed – the round world
in a minute;
Are all held still in the corridor of life.
Cut short – now – shot-through,
your footsteps remain and your footsteps
can still be heard.

For kings and princes, lovers and queens,
rich and poor – purveyors of dreams,
Set no flame, set no flame!
Let us lie together in the garden unchained.

Pictured with the Most Reverend & Right Honourable John Habgood, Archbishop of York at County Hall, Northallerton. The Archbishop is flanked by left Councillor K. Claire Brookes, OBE, a Deacon of Zion Church, Settle and Beth Graham right side, then Chair of North Yorkshire County Council, personal friends of the author, together with representatives of North Yorkshire County Council.

The 'Noah's Ark' window at St James' Church, Cross Roads, Haworth dedicated on the occasion of the marriage of Beverley Moore with the author. Here, on the inscription, a rarity, the author is addressed as the Reverend Mark Jones (Mark being the family name).

Evening Prayer

Night has fallen, Lord, night has fallen
The world is quietened from the strain of day

Touch with your hand this night
All those far from Thee; all those lost in fear

The poor, the oppressed, and those that cry
With unquenched tears in quiet rooms,

See through them all Lord, with your all-seeing eye;
Bless the little ones, the orphans far from home

Enstrengthen and empower the hands of all
Whose ministry it is to heal;

From the broken and the fragile, build anew
To the sleeping and the dormant heart

Waken faith in you;

Night has fallen, Lord, night has fallen
Grant us peace upon our homeward way;

Lead us to yourself, let us follow you
At break of day.

The late Right Reverend William Gordon Wheeler,
Bishop Emeritus of Leeds, a personal friend, on retreat at
Whitby, Summer 1996.

Sussex Prayer
A prayer for all seasons

God of all seasons
Whose changeless form and spirit pervades all,
Preserve us in our winters,
Defend us from all harmful thoughts and misdeeds,
When the storms of life o'ercome us
season us with your gift of health and joy and wonder,
Lift us when we are downcast,
Encourage us when we are sad,
Find us when we are lost,
Keep us from all that would make us doubt
Your never-failing help, and providence, and care.
                                        Amen.

Garlands of Hope from
Fields of Gathered Flowers

To A Rose

Flower of virtue
Flower of pain,
Flower of beauty
Praise, disdain,
Flower of my heart
Let your petals fall,
Flower of the green lea,
Flower of the wall,
Sweeten the path,
Sweeten the fall,
Flower of the sunshine,
Flower of the rain,
Bloom of the sun and thorn of the flame,
Saviour of hope and crown of all kings,
Flower of victory, flower of peace,
Mistress of meadow
Gracing our dreams,
Touched by the wonder. . .
Caught by the light,
Scent by far greater sense than our sight,
Speaking in silence, flower of night,
Flower of brightness, flower of day,
Joy of my life, my strength and my stay,
Flower of virtue, flower of pain,
Flower of love,
In my garden remain.

The Flying Dove
(To Beverley)

How do I try to explain the love you give to me?
You do it in special ways and indescribably,
The special note, the careful thought,
The sheer surprise – lies in your eyes!
The sudden way you lift my spirits,
And push my faith beyond its limits,
The laughs, the tears, the joy, the love,
And tenderness as fits the glove,
Patience, peaceful, quiet repose,
Soothes my heart and makes me whole
Strength to overcome the fear –
Is gathered-in when you are near,
Strength to rise again, and say,
We will live our lives – we have won the day;
Together forever – we will find a way,
So take my hand and share my love,
As wings befit the flying dove.

Pictured at the induction service at Shotts E.U. kirk with left to right, the Reverend Matthew Sullivan, MBE, the Reverend John Butler, the Reverend John Owain Jones and centre Pastor Graham Adams. (Photo: Courtesy of Wishaw Press.)

To Beverley

You are my life –
My constant thought,
You are my dream come true,
You make me realize the power of good,
And teach me how to trust anew.

You crown my life with all that's true,
And honourable and fair,
With you I love to share my hopes
And share a laugh awhile.

So let us always be together
In each other's arms,
My first, my last,
My joy, my love,
No peace have I without you.

Love Inseparate I

I miss you more than words can say
when we are apart,
I love you more than there are hours
in a day,
Great yawning gaps, though short,
seem like years,
I live and breathe to see you and be
with you,
And nothing else will do!
When I am alone – the chasm hurts my
heart . . .
And I am only half the person I can be.

Pictured with wife Beverley and Samuel in Shotts E.U. kirk, April 2000. (Photo: Courtesy of Nigel McBain, Motherwell.)

Love Inseparate II

When with you – united – fears dispelled,
Clouds disappear,
You take my hand and guide me
to the brightest dawn,
Out of darkness, out of sorrow,
out of tears,
Faith, hope, love – NEW LIFE –
is here to stay,
When I am with you – and you are with me
Inseparate
That immortal day.

Spring Harvest
Easter, 1998

I looked out upon fields of corn
Dark and handsome –
glistening with the dawn;

A kind of resurrection held its sway,
from fields of lambs and gathered flowers
the touch intrinsic – far beyond all mortal powers.

He spake,
thus spake,
the 'Voices of the hours' –

'True love can never be replaced,
Its memory lives with us still –
it can never be effaced;
Stronger than the human heart
than death itself –
An unknown, awesome, fresh experience,
green in root and palm;
An endless April morning –
filled with hopes of Spring.'

Illustration of Shotts E.U. kirk by J. Wigg.

Celtic Tides

The Shorrun of Shotts

What giant steps have formed this land
That from Hartwood to Torbothie spans?;
Dykehead, Springhill, Stane, they are but names,
Though whole communities grew up on abandoned hills;
Yet joys and tears are ours who share the common lot,
And labour on in love's lost little plots
Of terraced villas, homely Shotts.

There are divisions, aye, but none too deep,
For greater things unite us than divide;
Friends holding hands and hearts open wide,
We are climbing all the time and leaving fast behind
Old days of steel and iron and coal,
Brave memories of the mind;
Barren, gaunt and bred of sterner stuff,
We are rising from the darkness,
The brokenness of time – spent in toil and graft and hardship,
Sacrifice for what you find.

But crosses stand across this glen
And point us to the skies;
The kirk, the chapel, the Mission Hall,
The 'fire and blood' of men;
Not for want of virtue, lack of gain,
The hands that clasp the bars, clasp not in vain,
Nor walls divide the centuries from the stars.

What stories they have told me of Fortissat, sanctuary, and
Covenanter's book,
Where is the soul immortal – that lost time and legend took?
From far flung greener bowers we are born,
To dark and brooding grand elysian towers;
Hands frozen in time, petrified and powerful,
Hold a future such as ours;
Dreams of E.U. Church, the Kirk o'Shotts – no ivory towers!

Ahead of many a gravestone – a grim reminder to us all,
That death comes far too easily
For those forgotten by the storm;
What mortals lie beneath this earth of Benhar and of Stane?,
Whom once were bred and born in Shotts,
Now shelter from the rain;
And yes, we know there are fairer vales,
But, beauty is cruel and then is kind;
Rugged rocks, moorlands, mining hills now green again,
Can say, some say, more,
Still witness to a different kind of gem,
The fruit of labour with a lamp, an axe and such as like.

Yet, sing again of passion, love and aye,
The spirit of the time that passed us by,
A shinty and a 'shorrun' of Shotts will always make us cry:
'Hail bonnie brae, still bonnie stay;
Lassy, wee lassy, we ken you're away,
Away with the trees, away with the birds,
In Shotts we will find you,
Away and away'.

We are rising from the blackness,
What we find is peace of mind,
For that which shines is that which guides
And leads us from our fears,
The many-sided avenues that led us down the years,
O God let us find it in our hearts to be the better-minded,
Since what Shotts will show to us all again is
In death we are not divided.

Wales, My Wales

Wales, my Wales,
Rugged, desperate – alone,
A 'mercy seat' – a gospel throne,
Brooding with beauty,
Tainted with toil,
Land of hard-won victories,
Of raging mountains
Echoing unworldly cries.

Whose heritage is carved out
From above as below.
Deep in your valleys
Children play
As each new day
A monument is laid,
Another headstone for yet another grave
For one more tired brother of the night,
Whose misspent life in the dark avenues of strife
Might be another flower 'born to blush unseen',
Though many may feel the warmth and burn the light
Of your black days beneath the Tillery.

Harken once more to the tumbling falls
Of Llyn Ogwen, Aber and Porthlwyd,
See now in visions the golden bays,
Malldraeth, Rhos, Tremadog, Cardigan,
All beautiful and wise with age,
Caernarvon shining with its castle grand,
All bold examples of this strange, enchanted land.

Wales, my Wales,
Your chapels ring rejoicing at the love that you have shown,
Sheltering the weary seamen in your harbour's 'home from home',
The spirit of the heroes and their havens wait for all,
Arthur's Quoit and Baron's Hill,
Moel Hebog, Llaneilian
Whisper of your kings and princes,
Of Owen Glendower, Gryffyth ap Cynan,
Maelgwyn, Gwynedd and Llewellyn.

Let me wander through your wild and wooded glens,
May the summer never, never end,
What need has man when he has you for friend?
O, beauty, beauty that is Wales, my Wales,
From the North to the South – hear the melodies that are played,
Even in your darkest vales – families gather to sing your praise,
Recognition of the power that prevails
In all who live and love this Wales, my Wales.
This is your anthem . . . prayer,
Timeless as the rock of Cader Idris . . . Snowdon fair,
Boundless and eternal as are all your saints,
O, mystical adventure that is
Wales, my Wales.

Cherished Mantles,
Open Doors

St Valentine
(The Sacred Heart)

And still the door remains open
  despite all we say and do
And still the door remains open
  a never ending view
Love's richest colours blending
  with nature's cruellest hue
And still the door remains open
  no locks or chains to bind
The fainting heart finds courage
  and sight given to the blind
And still the door remains open
  no barriers can be found
The heart that bleeds forgiveness
  and healing of the mind . . .
And still the door remains open
  a vessel broken with time
The key has already opened
  the gates flung open wide
And still the door remains open
  love beckons 'come inside'
And still the door remains open
  the kingdom lies behind
And still the door remains open
  for always and for ay.

Anniversary, 2000

Love sleeps sweet
While many a vain tear
is passed at the harvest of a year,
Another year has come and gone
But, love sleeps on,
Carrying flowers as she goes
Touching lightly our repose
Love sleeps sweet,
Love immortal, love divine,
Arm on shoulder, hand in mine
Leads me through another door
The dance is over, cross the floor

Love is leading us still
To a finer place than this,
Your heart and my heart
Only she can fill,
Bedecked in branches of the eternal vine
Beauty dies, but virtue outlives time,
Love sleeps sweet
Yet, mortal dreams remain
Her lips to kiss the eyelids of the blind,
Love sleeps sweet
And she will shine
Awake to find the memory of some forgotten shore,
To pass across the mantle through that door

Love sleeps,
Love sweetly sings
'I have gone before, I know all things
You know me now, as you knew before'
Love sleep sweet,
Love sleep still,
Conquering all our human will.